Mary had a Dinosaur

First published 2007
Evans Brothers Limited
2A Portman Mansions
Chiltern Street
London W1U 6NR

Text copyright © Eileen Browne 2007
© in the illustrations Ruth Rivers 2007

British Library Cataloguing in Publication Data

Browne, Eileen
    Mary had a dinosaur. - (Twisters)
    1. Dinosaurs - Pictorial works - Juvenile fiction
    2. Children's stories - Pictorial works
    I. Title
    823.9'14[J]

ISBN-10: 0 237 53341 3 (hb)
ISBN-13: 978 0 237 53341 0 (hb)
ISBN-10: 0 237 53337 5 (pb)
ISBN-13: 978 0 237 53337 3 (pb)

Printed in China

Series Editor: Nick Turpin
Design: Robert Walster
Production: Jenny Mulvanny

Mary had a Dinosaur

Eileen Browne
and Ruth Rivers

Evans

Mary had a...

...dinosaur,

with horns...

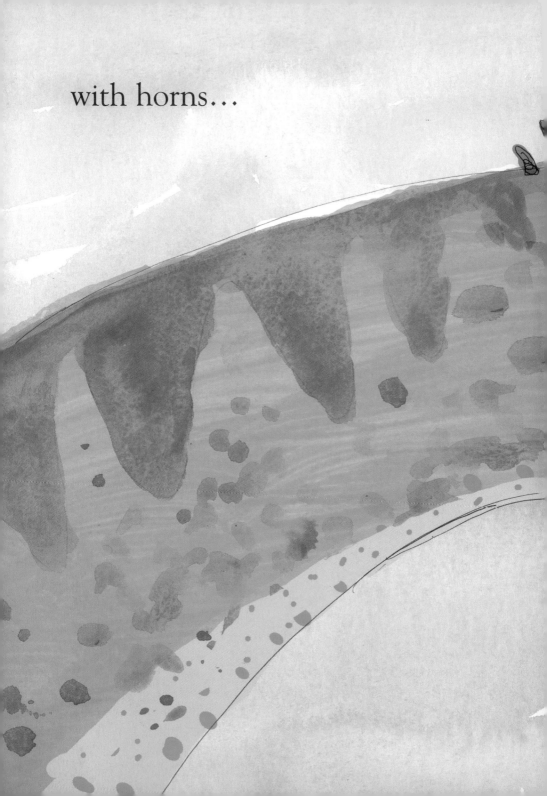

...and spotty knees.

It shared her lunch,

it pushed her swing…

...it helped her climb some trees.

It followed her…

...to school one day.

The children said,

25

It made the children laugh…

...to see a dinosaur...

...in school!

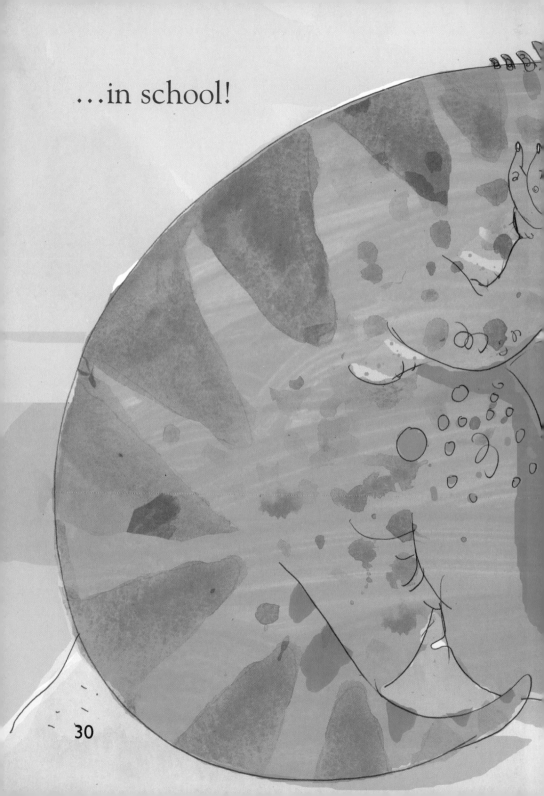